MADELINE'S CHRISTMAS

MADELINE'S CHRISTMAS

By Ludwig Bemelmans

VIKING

Sincere thanks to Mrs. Ludwig Bemelmans and Barbara Bemelmans for their help
and advice in adapting and restoring the text and art for *Madeline's Christmas*,
and for lending us the few remaining pieces of original art.
For this book. the art has been photographically enlarged and recolored by Jody Wheeler
to prepare it for reproduction.

VIKING

A Division of Penguin Books USA Inc., 375 Hudson Street, New York, New York 10014
Penguin Books Ltd. Harmondsworth. Middlesex. England
Penguin Books Australia Ltd. Ringwood. Victoria. Australia
Penguin Books Canada Ltd, 10 Alcorn Avenue, Toronto, Ontario, Canada M4V 3B2
Penguin Books (N.Z.) Ltd. 182–190 Wairau Road. Auckland 10. New Zealand

Originally published as a special book insert in the 1956 Christmas edition of *McCall's*

This edition first published by Viking Penguin Inc. 1985
Published simultaneously in Canada

ISBN 0-670-80666-8
Library of Congress Catalog Card Number: 85-40092

Manufactured in U.S.A.
Set in Bodoni

10

MADELINE'S CHRISTMAS

In an old house in Paris

That was covered with vines

Lived twelve little girls

In two straight lines.

They left the house at half-past nine

In two straight lines, in rain or shine.

The smallest one was MADELINE.

She was not afraid of mice
She loved winter, snow and ice
And to the tiger in the zoo
Madeline just said...
"POOH, POOH!"

It was the night before Christmas
And all through the house
Not a creature was stirring
Not even the mouse.

For like everyone else in that house which was old
The poor mouse was in bed with a miserable cold.

And only
Our brave little Madeline

Was up and about

And feeling

Just fine.

Suddenly came a knock
Which made her pause—

Could it perhaps be Santa Claus?
But no…

A rug merchant was at the door.
He had twelve rugs, he had no more.

"Why, these," said Madeline, "would be so neat
For our ice-cold in the morning feet."

"It seems to me," said Miss Clavel,
"That you have chosen very well."

Madeline gave him a handful of francs,
"Here they are with all our thanks."

Without the rugs
Which he had sold
The rug merchant got awfully cold..

"To sell my rugs," he cried, "was silly!
Without them I am very chilly."
He wants to get them back—
But will he?

He made it—back to Madeline's door—
He couldn't take one footstep more.

And little Madeline set about
To find a way to thaw him out.

The merchant, who was tall and thin
(And also a ma-gi-ci-an)
Bravely took his medicine.

The magician, as he took his pill, said
"Ask me, Madeline, what you will."
Said she, "I've cooked a dinner nutritious,
Will you please help me with these dishes?"

"If you'll clear up
I'll go and see
If I can find
A Christmas tree."

His magic ring he gave a glance
And went into a special trance—
The dirty dishes washed themselves
And jumped right back upon the shelves.

And then he mumbled words profound—

"ABRACADABRA"
BRACADABR
RACADAB
ACADA
CAD
A!"

That made the carpets leave the ground—

And twelve little girls were on their way—

To surprise their parents on Christmas Day.

Miss Clavel again quite well
Thought it time to ring her bell
Which quickly broke the magic spell.

And now we're back, all twelve right here
To wish our friends a HAPPY NEW YEAR!